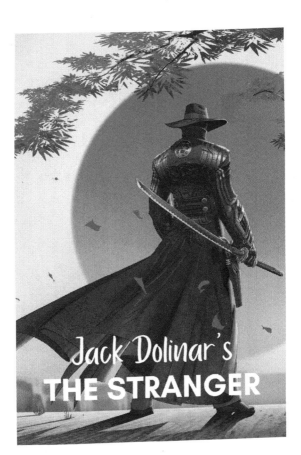

Jack Dolinar's
THE STRANGER

THE STRANGER

JACK DOLINAR

For Belle. Thank you for believing, encouraging and inspiring.

CONTENTS

THE STRANGER

The stranger looked worn, but not tired.

He wore worn boots, the kind that have been walking for a thousand miles. He was wrapped in a worn cloak, made of faded fabric from distant lands. He carried a worn sword, the kind that has never been hung over a mantle piece. Only his eyes were new. Like bright pennies, or the sun shining suddenly on your face.

That was how the stranger arrived in the town called Josek. This was 5,000 years after humankind had gone back to dust.

The sheriff's deputies put the stranger in quarantine for seven days. They took everything he had worn, but they couldn't take those bright penny eyes. They wished they could. The eyes were what worried them the most.

***

The way you see the world is always new and ever changing. It can never be taken away, and that is why it contains your power.

THE SHERIFF OF JOSEK

The sheriff of Josek carried a gun. This made her powerful.

She carried her power in the set of her hips and shoulders. She sat like a panther in her office, smoking. She carried her power in the dark ocean of calm that surrounded her, and in her tempest blue eyes. Her ebony face looked proud with power, and stern like old towers.

This was what the stranger saw when the sheriff's deputies dragged him in.

He forgot it all when she began to speak, and he learned what her power looked like on the inside.

Learn to draw conclusions from the inside out, instead of from outside in.

THE VAGABOND

G erardo was a long, rangy man. He had long, black hair to his shoulders, hanging in strands like raven feathers. His voice was long and forlorn.

Gerardo was a strange man. Everyone knew that. He was a traveler and a vagabond. Everyone could see it.

Except for the stranger, when the deputy sheriffs of Josek opened the door to the quarantine quarters and tossed him in.

The stranger felt naked without his boots and his cloak and his sword. The deputies had taken them.

"Hello," Gerardo said from across the room. His head was a little cocked to one side as he stood up.

His grin was a little bit empty. "Do you want to be my friend?"

The stranger looked at him for a minute without getting up off the floor. His eyes were bright as a candle in the abyss. He looked around the empty cement bunker.

He stood up.

"I believe I could use a friend," the stranger said.

Try to recognize when circumstances offer you what you need. It might not look like what you expected.

THE UNDERSTANDING

When the stranger met the sheriff of Josek for the second time she was lounging back in her chair with her boots up on the desk. There was a view out her windows of pockmarked mountains where nuclear missiles had once rained down like the fury of the gods.

The stranger's boots were also on the desk, standing upright. His sword was there, and his cloak in a heap.

"Am I free to go?" he asked.

"No reason to keep you in quarantine any longer," she told him. "So long as you make no trouble, you're free to pass through Josek and the surrounding territory."

"Thank you." The stranger went to pick up his be-
longings.

"However," she said. "If you do make trouble..." She
trailed off and her hand was nowhere near the butt of
her revolver.

The stranger nodded. "Naturally."

Not everything has to be said.

THE TROUBLE HUNTER

T he sheriff was waiting for the stranger on the road out of town. She sat astride a dirtbike that was covered in scars like an old war horse. Her riding leathers were deep purple.

She gestured with her half-finished cigarette. "You had copper pennies stashed in your boots," she said. "Enough to buy passage out of here. Maybe as far as Ghenkis. Why did you come all this way to Josek instead?"

The stranger shrugged. He kept walking.

The sheriff grabbed his arm. "Are you looking for something?"

She glanced at his sword when she said it. It was a worn sword, like the gauchos and swordslingers used when they dueled each other in the streets. But there were symbols chiseled in the blade that she had seen when the sword was on her examination table.

Not many were left who could read these symbols. The sheriff could. Her grandmother had been a tetric priestess and rune healer.

"Yes," the stranger admitted. He had seen her glance. She knew what he was. Or thought she did. "I'm looking for something. In the mountains beyond Josek."

The sheriff frowned. "The old tunnels go deep," she warned. "There's nothing good to be found up there."

The stranger smiled for the first time. His eyes glinted like those very same copper pennies.

"I'm counting on it."

⇛ ⇚

If you go looking for trouble, you'll probably find it.

THE UNEXPECTED TEACHER

The stranger was four days out of Josek and up into the mountains when Gerardo found him.

The raven-haired vagabond came shambling out of the shadows and into the firelight.

"Hello," he said. "Remember me? We met back in Josek. In the jail cell."

"How did you find me?" The stranger was sharpening his sword. He had heard Gerardo coming.

"The sheriff let me out yesterday morning." Gerardo scratched behind one ear. "She said maybe you had been going up this way, so I had a looksie and here you are."

The stranger raised his eyebrows. "You came all this way in a day?"

It had been hard hiking to get here. The landscape was bleak. Beyond Josek, the dirt was dry and broke apart between your fingers. The trees were brittle and stunted. The air burned in your nose. It had taken the stranger four days to get this far.

Gerardo shrugged. His weathered expression looked almost bashful. "I've been walking about in these hills since I was a boy."

The stranger nodded. "Alright. Tomorrow, you lead the way."

The next day, Gerardo began teaching the stranger how best to cross this shattered land.

There is always more to learn from each other.

THE SPECTER

It was a cold, overcast morning and the stranger was mending his cloak when he saw the specter.

He and Gerardo were up in the high places beyond Josek, where the mountains were crippled and sick. Five thousand years ago, many humans had built survival compounds in these mountains. The stranger doubted any of them had survived the nuclear barrage that came down from on high.

He saw the specter through the trees.

She looked like she had been beautiful once. Now she was pale and ethereal, beyond beauty and beyond life. She beckoned to him.

The stranger rose slowly to his feet. The cloak and sewing needle slipped through his fingers.

Come with me, her voice whispered in his thoughts. Her translucent fingers twitched and plucked at his emotions. She tugged his heart to compassion and to curiosity.

The stranger was closer now.

She held out a hand. *Come with me,* she whispered. *Leave that mortal body behind. Walk with me through the afterlands. There is no wind here. No thunderous death.*

The stranger reached toward her in a trance.

The specter's fingers curled like claws in anticipation.

Gerardo's crossbow twanged loudly.

His bolt, tipped with obsidian, punched through the specter's outstretched hand and then her chest. It spat out the back in a spray of dry leaves and spiderwebs.

The stranger flinched away, ripping his sword from its scabbard as he stared around wildly.

But the woman had vanished.

All that was left was Gerardo's arrow, buried halfway in the trunk of a bloated white tree. All around it, the bark had been charred black in the shape of a strange, spiderweb symbol.

Gerardo shook himself like a dog and left the bolt where it was. "Ghost," he muttered.

Maybe, thought the stranger. *But it was human once.*

In the end, temptations prove to be hollow.

THE CRATER LAKE

There was a crater lake way back in the mountains beyond Josek. Its color was a bright, unnatural blue that did not match the sky.

Gerardo sat on the mountainside looking down at the lake while the stranger scrambled up and down the rocks. The stranger kept glancing at a piece of paper that had been sewn into the lining of his cloak.

At last, hidden behind scraggly vines, the stranger found what he was looking for. It was a blast door, weathered with age and scarred by the same missile that had left behind the crater thousands of years ago.

Consulting his paper, the stranger punched a code into the ancient keypad.

The door slid open, releasing a wave of stale air.

Gerardo's eyes were wide. He gripped his crossbow.

The stranger drew his old, worn sword. "You have been a good friend," he said. "But this is my quest. I will not ask you to join me in pursuing it."

Gerardo watched the stranger go and wondered if he was brave enough to follow.

⟫⟫⟫ ⟪⟪⟪

Knowledge is the key, but you still have to step through the door.

THE TUNNELS

The creature leapt for his throat, chittering madly.

The stranger pinned it to the wall with his sword.

It was a mutant thing, with many legs and chitinous armor. It had a sting like a scorpion, as long as his arm.

Ancient, solar-powered lights fizzled in the deep, concrete tunnel. The stranger's copper eyes glinted in the dim light. He could see better in the dark than any human.

There had been many dead here. So many dead. All killed by the nuclear siege that had split open the mountains above them, or killed soon thereafter by the seeping sickness that spread through the tunnels.

If they survived the sickness, they did not survive what came next. The violent deaths of ten thousand souls and the savaging of the earth had torn open a hole in reality itself. Deep in the roots of these mountains, where survival bunkers had been carved into the living rock, twisted energies swirled together in a whirlpool.

What came through that pool was not of this realm. It was what the stranger had sworn to destroy.

The stranger ripped his blade free from the wall and beheaded the creature.

He hummed a sacred canticle as he went on, warding off the shadows.

⇶⇶ ⇷⇷

Be careful what doors you open. They can be hard to shut.

THE WHIRLPOOL GATE

B eneath the wasted mountains on the other side of Josek, far from the only remnants of civilization that still clung to this irradiated continent, the stranger fought for his life.

His worn sword was covered in gore. His threadbare cloak was spattered with blood. Exhaustion made his old boots heavy on his feet. He had been in the tunnels for days.

Wave after wave they came at him: the gibbering, chittering, mad creatures. They crawled through the whirlpool gate beneath the mountains and into the ancient survival bunkers that had been carved from the rock long ago.

This was where the stranger faced them.

The whirlpool gate was a shattered barrier between this realm and another, far more twisted, world. It was a gate the stranger had sworn he would close.

But there were too many of them, and in the shadowed silence between flashes of bloody combat the stranger made his decision.

By the time the next pack of gangly, howling mutants bounded up concrete stairs from the deep and cast about for his scent, the stranger was gone.

Recognize when it's time to regroup and reallocate your resources.

THE NEW SHERIFF

When the dark-skinned woman came to Josek, there was no sheriff. There was a man with a gun who ruled the town.

The man's name was Harrow. He paid bloody tribute to the power that lived under the mountains, and that power spared the town from its wrath. For a time.

When the woman came to Josek, Harrow's men brought her to him. She was beautiful, and Harrow was the kind of man who collects beautiful things. He kept her for months before she had her chance.

She took Harrow's gun after killing him with a letter opener. It was a violent day in Josek when she picked up

that gun, but when the day was over the ones who had
made her suffer were dead.

And there was a new sheriff in town.

The power under the mountains was a slow, seeping
kind of evil. But when it realized its servant was dead it
began to contrive its own plans for the town of Josek.

**Eliminating one problem only reveals the next. Be
ready. Stay vigilant.**

THE POSSE

The stranger fled the survival bunker with the hordes of hell chasing him.

The creatures scrambled over each other in the darkness, baying like dogs and gibbering like the insane.

He ran and ran, tripping over stones and floundering in the crumbled soil. At the crest of a low hill, he met Gerardo and the sheriff of Josek leading a ragtag group of deputies.

The sheriff swung down off her battle-scarred dirtbike. She was wearing her purple riding leathers and carrying a machete. Her gun was in its holster at her hip.

"Gerardo says you went down into the mountain days ago. I put together a posse. Looks like you're still alive."

The stranger nodded.

"Did you find what you were looking for? Did you kill it?"

That was when they heard the baying of his pursuers for the first time.

"They're angry," the stranger said. "And hungry."

The sheriff scowled. "Then this is where we stop them," she said, and set about making a battle line.

Help each other. Whatever it takes.

THE HILL

The sheriff of Josek and her deputies set up their battle line on a low hill. Gerardo stood in the back with his heavy crossbow. The stranger, panting from the chase, shook sweat from his eyes and wiped his bloody sword on the grass.

Marlin Tokas, chief deputy, said, "Here they come."

The creatures that swarmed up the hill toward them were covered in scabs and open sores, with limbs in the wrong places and slavering jaws full of teeth. Their claws were hooked and savage. They had come through the whirlpool gate under the mountains to ravage this world.

The stranger had tried to stop them alone. But he just made them angry.

Gerardo's crossbow spat an arrow into the pack. Somewhere, one of the creatures howled in pain. Then, they were all howling and leaping and slashing, crashing into the battle line in an explosion of tearing claws and fur and twisted screams that were nearly human.

Gerardo's crossbow twanged again.

The stranger swung his sword with furious might, taking heads and limbs.

Marlin Tokas was tackled to the ground and his throat ripped out.

The sheriff's gun barked, taking revenge.

It was a long few moments of chaos on the top of that hill.

~>>>>> <<<<~

Face the challenge. Make the sacrifice. You chose this moment. Keep on going.

THE ALLIANCE

W hen the fight was over, seven fresh graves had to be dug on top of that hill in the lands beyond Josek. They buried their own dead, but burned the bodies of the creatures they had killed.

Acrid smoke drifted on the breeze.

The sheriff of Josek came to where the stranger stood under a tree looking back at the mountains. The stranger had gone into those mountains to end a great evil. He had come back out with hell and death on his heels.

"You couldn't do it alone," the sheriff said. "And good men died for it."

The stranger nodded. He already felt the weight of their sacrifice on his shoulders.

"Next time," she told him, "I'm coming with you."

It's not too late. Maybe you just need another plan. Or a new ally.

THE COMRADES

The stranger traveled to Ghenkis to find comrades foolish enough to join him.

"In the mountains beyond Josek," he said, "there is a place where chaos and evil touches our world. The spawn of this place are hungry. The ruler of this place lusts for destruction. I need help to stop them."

But everywhere he went people turned aside. They had their own troubles, five thousand years after the fall of man. The only ones who listened to him were a young scholar from the Old College, a witch from across the sea, and a drunken fireman.

The scholar said, "I've read about this place and this evil. Maybe it's time to write a new history."

The witch said, "It is in the bones. This is my destiny."

The fireman knocked over his bottle on his way to the door. "Let's make them burn."

Accept what you are given. Often, it is exactly what you need.

THE CAMPFIRE

"What is a demon?" asked the fireman named Dolf, taking a swig from his bottle. He was a hulking shadow by the edge of the campfire. "What is it really?"

The young scholar pulled his candle closer. There was a battered book propped open on his knee. His name was Adain.

"There are records of demons from Before the Catastrophe," Adain said. "References in almost every one of the old religions. They are creatures of chaos and the dark, warped reflections of the angels and demigods. But what we call demons now are not the same. Our demons are real, tangible monsters that come from a reality totally unlike our own. They are not hellish, not divine, just mad and hungry. And our research at the college has turned up nothing at all about angels."

Shri Yazi, the witch, was stroking her raven familiar in the shadows. "Read all that in your books, did you?" she asked. "Have you ever met a demon, boy? We do not understand them. Not even the ones that used to be human. My folk call them the Gizthani, the Other Hunters, and while I've faced and banished my fair share I'm not pompous enough to pretend I know their story."

Adain gripped his book defensively. "See here—" he began.

But Dolf had already grown bored. "All I want to know," he said, taking another swig, "is if demons burn." The fireman stretched out his hand, and in response the campfire roared higher.

"They burn," said the stranger.

All three turned to face him. He was the one who had brought them together. The stranger with his worn sword, weathered cloak and weary boots.

"They burn. And they bleed. And together we will bring blood and fire to their very gate."

The stranger said nothing more. He did not tell them what he knew of demons. Or what he knew of angels.

⋙ ⋘

Seek challenges that fit your skill set. Find allies who fill the gaps.

THE BONES

Every night on the journey from Ghenkis back to Josek, Shri Yazi, the witch, threw the bones. Her raven familiar hopped among them, turning some over with his beak and helping her to read.

"There will be violence tomorrow," Shri Yazi declared one night, as they were crossing the Plains of Kador. Her raven croaked in agreement. "We will be attacked on the road."

Dolf, the fireman, took a swig from his bottle. "Good," he rumbled. Since the death of his wife and daughter, Dolf was a seeker of violence. Only his faith kept him from suicide.

Adain snorted and rolled his eyes. The young scholar had read about witchcraft at the Old College. He knew everything he needed to make a judgment.

The stranger just took out his worn sword and settled it across his knees. With long, careful strokes of the whetstone, he began to sharpen.

It never hurts to be prepared.

THE SCHOLAR'S LIES

A dain did not write the treatise that earned him his position as the youngest tenured professor at the Old College in Ghenkis.

It was penned by one of his graduate students, a brilliant theolomathematician named Garnice Frey. After she was tragically killed during a gang shootout in the Veda District, Adain kept her final term paper in a desk drawer for weeks as he debated what to do.

Then, over a cup of bitter coffee, the college provost informed Adain bluntly that if he didn't produce a spectacular piece of academia in the next few months he would be replaced by someone more suitably brilliant.

He rewrote Garnice's work and submitted it to universal acclaim. Instead of being let go, Adain was promoted.

But the lie plagued him.

When the stranger arrived in Ghenkis, speaking of an ancient evil lurking under the mountains beyond Josek, Adain jumped at the opportunity to leave the city behind him.

He thought, Maybe this will make up for what I've done.

But he knew it wouldn't.

⤜⤜⤜ ⤛⤛⤛

The choices we make in weakness will not fulfill us. They will haunt us, instead.

THE NEW ARRIVALS

The stranger, the scholar, the witch and the fireman arrived at the town of Josek in the shadow of the crippled mountains.

Adain, the young scholar, no longer had any doubts about witchcraft. Shri Yazi, the witch, had saved his life during a bandit attack on the Plains of Kador.

Dolf had been sober nineteen days. This did not improve the fireman's mood, but it made him six times as deadly.

Last night, after tossing and turning for hours, the stranger jolted awake from a nightmare to find that Dolf had made him a cup of soup.

They had come a long way since they first met in Ghenkis.

Their journey together had scarcely begun.

If the journey is worth taking, you will not arrive as the same person who left.

THE FAST FRIENDS

Gerardo met them coming up the main road into Josek. His hair was the same as before: long, matted and dark as the feathers of Shri Yazi's raven. His eye patch was new.

"She'll be happy to see you," he said to the stranger, meaning the sheriff. "It's been tough times since you left."

The sheriff was waiting for them in her office. She eyed the stranger's companions up and down with her hard, seasoned gaze.

Adain squirmed. Shri Yazi stared back. Dolf crossed to the bar and poured himself a drink, then stared at it like he was deciding whether another day sober was worth the effort.

"New friends?" the sheriff asked.

The stranger pursed his lips. When he first met his comrades in Ghenkis, they had been just a ragged band with common direction. But the harsh lands between Ghenkis and Josek made for fast friendships.

Adain followed Dolf, clapped the other man on the shoulder and took away the drink. He downed it himself, shuddering.

The stranger nodded. "New friends," he agreed. "And handy in a fight."

Gerardo flashed his daft, peculiar grin. "The best kind," he said.

⟫⟫⟫ ⟪⟪⟪

We become friends by standing together through all times.

THE SCHOLAR AND THE DARKNESS

There were many demons in the hills. The power under the mountain was growing stronger. The whirlpool gate — a hole ripped in the seams of this world — was spinning faster, opening wider.

The witch could feel it. So could the madman.

The stranger, the sheriff and the fireman cleared the way. The fireman spread his hands and left nothing but cinders behind.

Following in their bloody wake, the scholar looked with wide eyes on a place he'd only ever read about. It was a clear lake, bluer than the sky. It was a place where tens of thousands had died as they sought shelter in bunkers under the mountain.

The scholar knew that those deaths had unleashed something terrible from a reality beyond his own. He knew that when they reached the whirlpool gate, his learning could be key in closing it.

He did not relish the fight ahead. But he swallowed his fear and walked into the darkness. His friends were already ranging ahead.

***

Whatever happens, we cannot face it alone. We rely on each other, and we all have a role to play.

THE WHIRLPOOL GATE AGAIN

In the tunnels under the crippled mountain, what was once a network of survival bunkers had been overrun by monsters. Demons, they were called, though no one knew if that's what they really were.

The stranger and his comrades had not come to find out. They had come to kill.

Dolf the fireman flicked his wrist and bathed the tunnel ahead in a vortex of flames.

Demons gibbered and burned.

The company hacked their way through ancient concrete corridors to the very roots of the mountain.

The stranger had been here before, but without allies he had been forced to turn back.

In a pit behind a cracked and blackened blast door, the whirlpool gate frothed and spat. The power that made demons surged through this gate.

For hours, it seemed, they stood at the edge of that pit in the dark. They faced wave after wave of monsters and turned them back. But this was a gate without hinge or lock and no bars that would keep it closed for long.

Shri Yazi was the first to realize what must be done. They would have to find the source, somewhere on the other side. They would have to end this nightmare there.

With a cry, Shri Yazi's raven folded its wings and dove into the pit.

The witch opened her Third Eye and followed.

Don't turn back again. You'll find only familiar troubles. Making true change requires stepping into the unknown.

THE RAVEN

They followed Shri Yazi's raven down a tunnel that warped and curved, carving a bloody path between this world and another. There was no light here, just the distant flap of dark wings.

Flap. Flap.

Raw cosmic potential coiled and warped around them. Pure chaos unraveled the edges of their senses. Things came out of the dark and threw themselves on the stranger and his comrades.

The witch flexed her fingers and bound their foes in crackling lightning.

The stranger swung his worn sword and cut them down.

The scholar ducked his head and ran blindly, following the raven's wingbeat.

Flap. Flap.

They had come to close this passage for good, to protect the land that was their home. But first, they must escape this void between worlds.

Ahead, a sudden and blinding glow. A rift in the endless night.

Screaming, Gerardo covered his one good eye and fell to his knees. The sheriff of Josek grabbed him and dragged him through.

They burst into the light, into the land where demons come from.

Dark wings spread wide, the raven rose into the purple sky and screamed in triumph.

⇛⇚

When you don't know the way, pick one sign and follow it until you do.

THE LAND OF DEMONS

They fell through a hole in space and time like sand running from one globe of an hourglass into the other, the witch's raven guiding their way.

"This is the land of demons?" asked Dolf. The fireman's gruff voice sounded stunned.

The raven flapped around the clearing once and landed in a pale tree with blue, velvety leaves. The sky overhead was dusky purple shot through with streaks of pink and orange.

The sheriff of Josek tipped back her hat and sniffed the cinnamon-sweet air. She frowned and touched the revolver at her hip.

A small spring bubbled at the foot of the tree. The water was clear and twinkled like liquid diamond. The young scholar, Adain, stumbled to the spring and fell to his knees. He washed his face, then carried cool water to Gerardo, who twitched and trembled on the ground.

The stranger simply watched.

Shri Yazi, the witch, sidled up beside him. Her dark eyes met his bright copper ones through her hanging veil. "Where are we?" she demanded. "Where have you taken us?"

"To the land of demons," he finally answered. His voice came from far away. "Isn't it beautiful?"

⫸⫷

We really don't know where others are coming from until we go there and see for ourselves. Until then, we can only guess and judge.

THE FIREMAN

Dolf had waited a long time for revenge.

The fireman had been away from Ghenkis, fighting in the war against the Agoori Hordes. Alone among the scattered descendants of mankind, the Agoori consorted with ghosts, specters and demons, believing that the creatures had wisdom from beyond the veil of death.

Dolf was a member of the Fyr Tenne, a unit of firemen that was feared and hated by the Hordesmen. It was the Fyr Tenne who fought at the breach of Samaidh and drove back the Hordes, killing their warlord Dhruv Ajai and dozens of Agoori sorcerers.

Dolf himself had killed an Agoori witch as she carved her way through a squadron of Ghenkis militiamen, but with her last breath the witch had cursed him through bloody teeth.

"Gheb dro ghrad bas daemonia..."

"Your love will die by demons..."

The fireman had returned to Ghenkis to find his wife and daughter murdered in their beds. They had been locked in their home, tortured and torn apart. When the military police investigated the deaths they found bloody Agoori runes and evidence of demonic intrusion at the scene.

Dolf fell to drinking.

Then the stranger came to Ghenkis, offering a chance to close the doorway that brought demons into the world of men. Offering a chance at vengeance. Only now, they were in the land of demons itself, but for three days they trekked through the forest and saw not a soul.

At the edge of the woods, Dolf turned back. The liquor that had dulled his rage was left behind, and all the fireman had inside him was the urge to burn. His eyes glowed and liquid flame pooled in his palms. He raised a hand toward the pale trees.

The stranger stepped in his way. "Patience, my burning friend," he said. "This forest is no enemy of yours."

Adain, the young scholar, put a soothing hand on his big friend's shoulder. "Easy there..."

Dolf snarled and shrugged him off.

But even as he stalked away, he knew they were right.

When there seem to be no good choices, choose patience instead of anger.

THE GREY TOWER

They came to a sea, in the land of demons, where black cliffs plunged hundreds of feet to meet the churning water. Built on jutting rock above the cliffs, a mighty tower pierced the sky like a grey spear. The walls were of an alien metal that caught the light and shimmered like a mirage. At the foot of the tower was a huge, arched door.

The stranger approached, followed by the rest.

Dolf, the fireman, stared up at the tower with respect borne of military experience. "How're you planning to assault that?"

The stranger rolled up one sleeve and approached the access panel beside the door. "I know the way in."

"How do you know?" asked Shri Yazi, full of suspicion. The witch narrowed her eyes.

The stranger hesitated. Then, he placed one hand on the scanner and the massive door slid slowly open.

"Because," he said. "Long ago, this was my home."

The truth cannot remain hidden long. Sooner or later it will be revealed.

THE JURY

The stranger led them into the grey tower at the end of the sheriff's gun.

The sheriff of Josek, the scholar, the fireman, the witch and the madman all followed.

Inside, the walls were hung with holographic tapestries and lamps that spilled forth an unwavering blue light. The stranger showed them into the main hall, to a long table that could have seated a hundred guests with ease. He sat in a tall throne at one end, settling like a falcon in a familiar roost.

The sheriff sat a dozen chairs down the line. She set her revolver on the table, but kept it close. The stranger still had his worn sword at his side, and she had witnessed his deadly speed before.

"So," she said. Her stormy blue eyes dove deep into his copper ones.

"So..." he sighed.

Both had known this day would come.

The others were less reserved.

"Leading us into a trap, are you?" Dolf, the fireman, demanded. He slammed a fist down, and flames crackled across his knuckles. "Tell us we're coming here to hunt demons and all the while you were a bloody demon!"

"How can we possibly trust you, knowing what you are?" asked the scholar Adain.

Shri Yazi's tattooed face was grim. "I was born to kill demons," the witch said darkly. Her raven hopped along the back of her chair and croaked a dour echo.

The stranger watched the others, biding his time, waiting for their anger to run its course.

Gerardo bit his lip. He shared a look with the sheriff. "He has been a good friend to us," the madman spoke. "We fought together. He has not once betrayed us."

The sheriff grimaced. Her fingers tapped the grip of her revolver. Finally, she leaned forward on her elbows and jabbed a finger at the man who had led them here.

"It's time you spoke up," she told him. "For all our sakes."

The stranger nodded. "It's time you knew," he agreed. And when he told his tale, the others could not fault his secrecy. It was born of necessity, and age-old shame.

"Well then," said the witch.

"Alright," said the scholar.

"Fine," said the fireman.

They would trust the stranger. They would follow him to the end of this journey.

⤜⤜⤜   ⤛⤛⤛

Trust is what gives us courage to travel down new paths.

THE STRANGER'S TALE

The stranger spoke, from his ancient throne in that grey tower in the land of demons:

"For eons there was peace, an age of wisdom and reason for my people. The Praeds broke that peace when they arrived on this world from the darkness beyond the stars. Chaos, war, disease and madness were unleashed on our land.

"The leaders of the many houses were called together at the Field of Souls. There, the Empress demanded a monumental task. Half of us were dispatched in starships to find a new home. The rest would stay, and fight, and pray that the explorers would send for them.

"We traveled for years through the void of space. When we arrived at your homeworld, we thought we had finally found a safe harbor for our people. It was only then that our portalcallers revealed to us what was necessary: a massive missile barrage that would tear a hole in space-time, clearing the way for their magic to burrow a tunnel back home through the void.

"It had never been done before, but we could not hesitate. The future of our home, of our entire civilization, was at stake. No matter the cost, we had to save the ones who placed their faith in us.

"We pummeled the mountains with ordinance. Tens of thousands of your people died. Our portalcallers executed their ritual, but the strain drove them mad and swept them away. They were devoured in the darkness. Disaster.

"Then, from afar, my wartorn race heard the call. They saw the signs. They trusted in us. They found the whirlpool gate our portalcallers had opened. And then, our people came to us... their saviors.

"Only when they arrived here they were not the same. They were not safe in the void between the stars, for the portal was not complete. When they arrived in this new world, our people were warped and broken by the chaos they had traversed to get here. They were mad and hungry for peace, the peace they had sought for so long. It was a peace they now hunted. And devoured.

"It was not safe, but still they came, and when they arrived you called them demons. The fallout from our bombardment swept across the continent and powerful magic seeped in from beyond the gate. Together, these forces toppled your civilization.

"We had not simply failed. We had infected your world from the ruins of our own."

The stranger sat for many minutes with lowered head.

"I have been wandering your earth for five thousand years seeking peace. Seeking atonement. Seeking redemption."

He raised his face. He looked around at his companions.

"The time has come."

❯❯❯❯ ❮❮❮❮

The highest pursuits have the highest stakes, and can level the heaviest consequences.

The Purpose

There was an ancient craft at the top of the grey tower, dark like a stormcloud and sharp as an arrowhead. The stranger led them aboard.

In the cockpit, he swept his hand across the command console and an array of holocontrols flickered to life. Another gesture, and the craft rose smoothly into the air.

They crossed the sea in that craft, leaving the stranger's tower behind. Now that they knew the truth of their journey, the others watched the stranger warily.

"What do you suppose he wants, truly?" asked the young scholar. "Why is he so bent on saving our world, and destroying his?"

"Peace," said the fireman, who lived to escape his violent past.

"Freedom," said the witch, who lived to fulfill her epic destiny.

"Awk," said the raven, and the madman nodded agreement.

True peace is escaping the bonds of our past. True freedom is allowing an unknown future.

THE PRAEDS

N othing is more dangerous than an idea.

    If it is simple enough, an idea will multiply without end. If it inflames the passions, logic becomes helpless. Once it takes root, an idea is very hard to kill. Even banished, an idea can never die so long as someone is left to find it and bring it back to life.

The Praeds came to the stranger's home on a rock that plummeted from space. Their essence was carved in that rock. It was the seed of an idea, a virus of the mind that soon took root in their first host, the one who translated the ancient carvings.

At first, the Praeds were just an idea in one heart and one mind. Then, as they grew in numbers, the

Praeds took control of their host and began to spread. Like a psychic plague, they conquered and enslaved the stranger's world one heart and one mind at a time.

Five thousand years later, the stranger returned home to stamp them out once and for all.

Take care which ideas you host in your mind. They can elevate you, but they can also enslave you.

THE GRAND PLAN

"So," said the sheriff of Josek, joining the stranger in the cockpit. "You've been waiting thousands of years to return home. You must have a pretty good plan."

"No," said the stranger. His copper eyes watched the waves of the sea rippling past far below. He seemed almost unaware of her presence. "But when we arrive, I'll know what to do."

Sometimes you have to take the first step before the next one will reveal itself.

THE GHOSTS

They disembarked on a black sand beach and followed the stranger into the jungle.

The forest was lush and wet, climbing up the steep slopes of a rugged mountain range. They heard the rustle of trees in the wind, the rush of hidden streams and the pitter-patter of rain dripping down giant leaves. But though the place was rich with plant life, of animals there were none to be seen.

Shri Yazi's raven circled overhead and then returned to his mistress with a report.

"Where are the birds?" the witch asked. "And the jungle beasts?"

The stranger pushed back the hood of his old cloak. He cocked his head, as though listening.

"The Empress is calling," he said at last. "All creatures that can run, fly or crawl have answered." He grimaced. "We must move quickly. Even now, the trees are sending ahead word of our passing."

Their path wound up and up, higher into the mountains. Once, they came to a ridge and Gerardo looked back the way they'd come. But all he saw were mist and clouds gathering beneath them. He shuddered.

"What is it?" asked the sheriff of Josek.

Gerardo pushed his long, black hair away from his face. "I see ghosts in the mist," the madman admitted. "And they whisper that we will not return."

The sheriff shook her head. "Of course we won't return," she said. "We'll move on."

She climbed ahead, and, after one final glance back, Gerardo followed.

〰⟫⟫⟫ ⟪⟪⟪〰

When you reach the point of no return, move ahead. Be fearless.

THE MADMAN

Long ago, mothers kept the bedroom windows locked tight.

There were legends of fey creatures sneaking into nurseries by moonlight, bending over cradles and scooping infants up in their arms. They would steal away to the land of faeries, leaving behind an empty cradle and a bundle of twigs among the blankets. But those were legends of long ago, and when Gerardo was a baby the legends had been long lost.

It was the night of midsummer, and his mother had forgotten to lock the bedroom window.

Gerardo's earliest memory was of a pale face of unearthly beauty bending over him.

The next morning, his mother found a bundle of twigs in his cradle — holly, ash and alder, sprigs of the faery trees.

A year and a day passed.

Then, on a moonless night, Gerardo was returned to his nursery.

But now he was no longer a babe, for time passes differently in the other realms. He was a young man, with long, black hair like raven's feathers. And he was no longer sane.

Gerardo saw things, now. He heard things. He spoke to shadows and went out to wander in the hills beyond Josek, where ghosts and specters haunt the broken lands. He never spoke of what had happened. Perhaps he did not even remember. But he was never the same after that night.

His own mother did not recognize him, and would not look him in the eye. People shunned him. By the time the stranger came to Josek, Gerardo was all alone.

But the stranger was not afraid to look into Gerardo's eyes. And, when Gerardo looked back, he saw what ordinary mortals did not.

Gerardo saw that the stranger wore a burning crown of silver light on his brow. He saw golden runes inked on the stranger's scarred and weathered skin. He saw that the stranger's shadow was not human. He saw all of these things, and still he asked the stranger, "Will you be my friend?"

Truly, Gerardo was a madman. No one else could endure what he had, and still have a heart so open to friendship.

>>>>> <<<<<

We are all a little mad. We see things that others don't. And, if we're lucky, we act contrary to the conditions that try to control us.

THE FIELD OF SOULS

High in the mountains beyond the sea, they came through a narrow pass and looked out over a vast field. It was so broad that it stretched tot he horizon, bordered only by distant peaks.

The stranger had his old cloak thrown over one shoulder. He knelt and pressed a palm to the earth. His copper penny eyes looked down on the field. He saw endless rows of green stalks blanketed in soothing mist. He saw harvesters roaming up and down the rows, plucking eggs that would one day hatch into men like him.

"This is the place where I was born," he said.

The others looked.

But they did not see what the stranger saw. They saw a barren, grey husk of a place, full of blackened trees and spiderwebbed with vents that spewed foul gas. In the haze, menacing shadows flickered and hunted.

Time had not been kind to this place in the stranger's absence.

Everything we see is tinged by our perspective and our memory.

The Burning Orchard

Once, the Field of Souls had been a lush orchard. Year after year, high in the jungle-covered mountains, harvesters wearing warm cloaks had plucked eggs from the plants and gathered them in woven baskets. The eggs were carried to the foot of the Empress, laid out in hundreds of concentric circles, and the Empress herself watched over them until they hatched. One by one, she guided them out of their shells and into the light. Long ago, the stranger had been born here, at the foot of the Empress.

Then, the Praeds came.

At first, they were just an idea carved on an ancient rock that fell from the sky. But swiftly, like a virus, they spread through the hearts and minds of the Empress's people. That was how the Praeds became people. They took them over, one thought at a time. The Empress herself was the last to fall. The Praeds ate her from the inside out and took her power for themselves.

Now, the Praeds run the orchard. There are no harvesters in warm winter cloaks. Eggs fall from the trees in their time, and those that don't shatter are slowly cooked by the noxious heat that spews from cracks and vents in the dry ground. Some eggs hatch. What emerges is a true Praed, born from neglect and with an instinct for taking whatever it can to survive.

The stranger was tackled by one of these monsters as he stalked slowly through the withered orchard. The creature clutched his throat and wicked teeth snapped at his face. His sword was knocked from his hand.

Twang!

Gerardo's crossbow spat and the bolt buried itself in the monster's ribs. The stranger heaved the writhing body off him, snatched up his sword and beheaded it.

The sheriff of Josek helped the stranger to his feet.

He felt the deep weight of monumental sadness as his companions crowded round. He muttered a quiet prayer. Once, this had been the most sacred place in the world to his people.

"Dolf," he said. "This place is sick. It needs a cleansing fire."

The fireman grinned through his beard. "Fire, you say?" His eyes began to glow. Sparks whirled around his fingers. "With pleasure."

Dolf spread his hands.

Flames engulfed the blackened trees.

Move on from what something was in the past. Handle what it has become now.

THE WITCH

The Praeds had conquered the stranger's home like a virus. They had turned the Field of Souls into a spawning ground for monsters. They had defiled the Empress and bent her to their will.

Now, the Field of Souls went up in flames.

The stranger's company raced through the vast, burning orchard. They raced for a tall hill at the center of the Field, a hill surmounted by the largest tree any of them had ever seen. It towered over the orchard, great limbs stretching skyward and casting the hill in deep shadow.

This was the Empress.

At the foot of the hill, the stranger turned. Through the noxious clouds of vapor and swirling smoke, lanky, snarling creatures crept closer.

The stranger drew his old sword and looked to Shri Yazi, the witch. "I can go no further," he said. "I will buy you time."

The sheriff of Josek drew her revolver and machete. The fireman joined them in his long leather duster. Gerardo, the madman, prepared his crossbow.

"We will buy time," the madman said. "You must end the sickness."

Shri Yazi looked up the dark hill.

She had been training for this all her life. She remembered the rocky, rain-lashed islands of Av, where she was born. For thirteen years she was raised a witch, trained in potions and palm readings. Then, for thirteen years more, the coven taught her other skills: what some called "sorcery" and others "the deep science." They taught her to throw the bones and to read them, to know the future and to shape it. Shri Yazi was adept at reading the bones.

She remembered the day she read a fortune which drove her from her home, out into the world. It was the day she first saw the symbol of the Great Demon next

to the Tree of Life, and knew her destiny was to bring
down both.

Shri Yazi scrambled to the foot of the path. She left
her friends behind and began to climb.

Her raven, circling overhead in the thickening
smoke, swooped low and followed.

**Your past, every experience from start to finish,
has trained you for this opportunity. Only you can
face it. Climb the hill, and put that preparation to
use at last.**

THE EMPRESS

At the peak of a high hill in the Field of Souls, Shri Yazi the witch stood before the greatest tree she had ever seen. This was the Empress, the tree goddess of the stranger's world, who had been corrupted by the dark magic of the Praeds.

Smoke, ash and embers whipped through the air. The Field of Souls was ablaze. Screams and roars drifted up from the base of the hill, where the witch's comrades fought to buy her time. The stranger, the fireman, the sheriff and the madman, even the scholar remained behind.

Her raven, alone, was with her.

In a hollow between two huge, twisted roots, the witch could see a swirling vortex in the trunk of the tree. It was an entrance to the whirlpool gate, a portal that allowed the creatures of this blighted world to travel to hers.

It must be closed. The Praeds could not be allowed to spread.

Shri Yazi pressed her palm into the rough bark.

The Empress, bitter and corrupt, smote the witch with magic that was old as mountains.

With a cry, the raven swooped between them and took the blow.

The witch's shadow rose, spread like dark wings, and plunged into the heart of the tree.

There was silence.

Then, with a thunderous CRACK that echoed out over the burning Field, the trunk of the mighty tree split from its rotten core. The Empress tottered. She fell.

Between twisted roots, the whirlpool gate spun itself into nothing. No more madness would steal through.

The raven lay amid broken branches.

Shri Yazi was nowhere to be seen.

Our greatest works are greater than any one of us, alone. They are products of time, place and timing on a scale so large as to make the individual vanish. You may be the final puzzle piece, but, when the picture is complete, all the pieces disappear.

THE ESCAPE

The world mourned the death of the Empress.

Clouds gathered, and a cleansing rain began to fall over the Field of Souls. The raindrops quenched the fire that raged throughout the burning orchard.

In the Field itself, the stranger and his comrades fought desperately to escape. Shrieking Praeds chased them through the trees.

At the base of the mountain pass, Dolf the fireman blasted a boulder into rubble and slid several tons of stone across the path behind them.

"They'll be on us again soon," the stranger said grimly. He looked up at the mountain. "And we can't outrun them through the jungle."

"Where can we go?" Adain panted. The scholar was bleeding from a long cut down his face.

"Follow me," said Gerardo, who had never been here before. He scrambled up the slope.

The stranger, the scholar, the sheriff and the fireman all followed.

In a nook between two tall rocks, the madman showed them a green door, covered in moss and with a stone knob. He spoke to the door in a language none of them knew, and it opened.

Gerardo stepped through. His comrades followed.

When the Praeds tracked their scent to the two tall rocks, they found nothing.

The door had vanished.

When you can't see your way out of a problem, try following a crazy idea.

THE LAND OF THE FEY

I t was broody and dark in this forest. Muffled bird-calls echoed. Somewhere, they could smell a bog.

Gerardo told them they were in the land of the fey. The madman had lived here for a long time when he was young, and if he was lucky he could still find a door back to it in lonely, out-of-the-way places.

Adain, the young scholar, was still in shock after their battle at the Field of Souls.

The sheriff of Josek bandaged Adain's face and clapped him on the shoulder. "You'll be alright," she said gruffly. "Won't even lose the eye."

"What about Shri Yazi?" he mumbled.

Back at the Field, the witch and her raven had gone up the hill to face the Empress. But they had not returned.

Dolf, the fireman, put an arm around the scholar's shoulders. He had lost comrades before. "We'll raise a full pint in her name," he said. "And one for her bird, too."

Gerardo called back to ask if they were ready to move.

Adain swallowed and nodded.

"I'll be alright," he said. "We should keep moving."

Some things cannot be fixed immediately. You just have to wait a little while.

THE FOREST PATH

G erardo led the stranger's company through the murky forest of the fairy realm.

Once they heard distant music, but Gerardo guided them quickly and quietly away.

At a crossroads, they saw a knight with stag's antlers dueling a fire-breathing bear. A crowd of woodland creatures had gathered to watch. Here, they were noticed by a red fox, who watched them with narrowed eyes and then bounded away into the forest.

An hour later, Adain asked, "Where are we going? Do you even know where we are?"

Gerardo squinted around in the mist. He adjusted his eye patch from one eye to the other, and squinted around with his other eye. "Not sure," the madman grunted. "But this land always takes me where I need to go."

Not five minutes later, Gerardo found a lichen-covered door in the back of an old oak tree.

Again speaking in a language none of his comrades understood, he opened the door and they followed him through.

⤜⤜⤜ ⤛⤛⤛

Don't force things. Let them fall into place on their own.

THE PRICE OF THE PAST

T hey followed Gerardo through a door in the back of an old oak tree.

"Is this where you meant to take us?" asked Adain, the scholar.

Gerardo looked around. They were in a grove of tall, slender trees. Across the clearing of close-cropped grass sat a throne of woven branches. A smug red fox sat at the foot of the throne, and on the throne sat a beautiful, red-haired queen.

Gerardo went pale.

The queen spoke.

"Gerardo uses my doors, young Adain, but I choose where they lead. And today they lead you through my court."

"Who are you?" demanded Dolf, the fireman.

The queen smiled, rosy and warm like the dawn sun. "I am Brigidde, the Bright One. I have heard your tale from Aghma, our storyteller, and count it as good luck that you have chosen to return home through my kingdom."

She tilted her head.

"But Gerardo, my prince, you must stay behind. It has been ages since anyone as entertaining as you has graced my court. So naughty of you to try and escape..."

Dolf leaped forward to stop her, but the queen raised her hand.

There was a flash of cold, bright light.

Dolf stumbled and fell to his knees on the dusty main street of Josek.

They were home.

Gerardo was gone.

We don't always end up where we intended. Sometimes we end up where we were before, because now is the time to pay the price.

THE VICTORS

Now that the dark force under the mountains was gone, there were fewer and fewer monsters in the hills.

The town of Josek grew, but the stranger and his comrades — who had gone to hell and back to stop that force — parted ways.

The stranger remained only long enough to confirm that the whirlpool gate was indeed closed. Then he was off, trekking south towards the River Rioja.

Dolf, the fireman, left for Ghenkis. There, he re-enlisted and was deployed once more against the Agoori Hordes.

Adain stayed. They called him the Scarred Scholar, now, and he wrote books about space, time and travel between worlds. He started a school in town.

The sheriff of Josek got elected mayor of the prospering community, but it was hard for her to rely on her delegates and the town committees. She still carried her trusty revolver everywhere.

It was some time before the company came back together again.

꙳꙳꙳ ꙳꙳꙳

As times change, so do our circumstances. Embrace your new role.

THE LIZARD

One day in the course of his travels, the stranger saved a drowning man from the River Rioja.

While the man dried off by the fire, the stranger waded in the frigid shallows. With a small net, he fished out a bedraggled bumblebee and a red-bellied lizard.

The lizard was cold and stiff, so he placed it on a rock that had been warmed by the flames. After a few minutes, the lizard had thawed enough to scuttle away.

"What'cha do that fer?" asked the man. "Thing won't remember nuthin'. Won't even know you did it a good turn. Not like it's human."

The stranger shrugged. "I'm not human either."

He left it at that, and the man departed soon after,
looking over his shoulder as he went.

Life is precious, regardless of the form it takes.

THE LAST BONFIRE

D olf trekked north with his unit of firemen, burning and burying the Aghoori forces sent to stop them.

They drove deep into enemy territory. Dolf heard his captain say that they were looking for the source of Aghoori power, the sacred place that fueled their sorcerers' magic.

At a high place in the mountains, they came to a plateau of lush forest surrounded by snowy peaks on all sides. The air was humid and filled with sweet mist. Two of Dolf's unit were ensnared by specters and led away in the night. They did not return.

Half a day's journey into the mist, the firemen came to a hill crowned by a single, solitary sapling.

Dolf recognized the tree. He had seen its kind only once before, far away on the stranger's homeworld, in the Field of Souls. This one was far younger, but it bore an unmistakable resemblance to the Empress, the queen tree who had ruled over the stranger's world for millennia.

Dolf's captain wanted to burn it down immediately, but Dolf convinced her to wait. He harvested twigs, leaves and seeds from the tree before it went up in flames. As ashes rose on the breeze, the plateau was swarmed with Aghoori fighters.

Dark, winter magic rained down. Screaming warriors clad in furs charged through the mist and smoke. Dolf and his comrades summoned fire and fought them.

They were deep in the mountains, cut off from reinforcements and from retreat.

Dolf gave his captain what he had gathered. "Inez," he told her. "Bring these to Adain the scholar. In Josek. Promise me."

Then, blazing like a bonfire, Dolf went out and cleared the way for his comrades to escape.

>>>> <<<<

Recognize what is important to save and what must be burned.

THE SPELLSLINGER MAGE

The spellslinger mage came into town from the
other side of the mountains.

She had long, red hair and a blue cloak that had been
worn soft with time.

When the mage came to city hall with her doc-
uments and the two were introduced, the mayor of
Josek thought that the woman looked familiar. She had
bright, copper-penny eyes, like a stranger the mayor had
once known. The mage had a look about her that the
mayor recognized: a restless, dangerous look.

But the mayor said nothing. She just gave the mage a
firm handshake, went on her way, and later that after-

noon sent a message to the new sheriff saying that he should post a deputy to keep an eye on the hotel where the mage was staying.

Sooner or later, the mayor knew, that mage would be up to something.

Trust your intuitions and you will be ready for anything.

THE MEDICINE MAN

Several hundred miles south of the River Rioja, the stranger came to a small village in the jungle. He hired native guides, and they led him deep into the forest.

There, the stranger consulted with an old medicine man who had lived in solitude for decades.

"The villagers say that you are a true maya, or magician. That you can heal the sick and see the future. That you can walk between worlds."

The medicine man watched him carefully from the other side of a low fire. "You seek to enter the realm of the Tata Duende," he said. "The forest folk. The magical ones."

"I do," said the stranger.

The hermit threw a handful of leaves and bark onto the fire. Sweet smoke began to fill the thatched hut. "Why?" he asked.

"I left a comrade behind," said the stranger. "A friend. It's time I went and brought him back."

The smoke grew thicker.

"Breathe deep..." the medicine man instructed. "And go."

When the stranger staggered from the hut, his head was spinning. He lurched away into the jungle, eventually falling against a huge, broad-boughed tree. Opening his eyes, the stranger saw, to his amazement, that there was a rough, geometric door carved into the bark.

But he didn't question it.

Like he had seen his friend Gerardo do in the past, the stranger pulled open the portal and stepped through into the land of the fey.

It was time to save his friend.

Friends go back for each other.

THE GOOD COALS

A dain had a small, wood-burning stove in his office at the academy.

Every morning during the cold, frontier winters of Josek, Adain stoked the fire before settling back behind his desk to prepare his lessons. On good mornings, there was still a bed of glowing coals from the previous night. These coals needed only a few moments of coaxing to wake back up into a cheery blaze.

Days like these, Adain remembered his friend Dolf, the fireman. Firemen can summon flames from nothing, but Dolf taught Adain to cherish every ember.

Let a fire die, Dolf said, and you have to create it again from nothing. Let it rest, and you can rely on it to endure and revive, day after day.

On the morning that the spellslinger mage came to his office, Adain had been sitting and staring into the stove for a long time. Lost in thought, the only thing he'd written was a scrawled note across the top of one of his papers.

"We are so much like these flames."

All of us eventually burn to ashes. Some of us leave good coals behind.

THE RESCUE

B rigidde, the Bright One, a queen in the land of
the fey, was seated on her throne when the red fox
came in. Gerardo was curled up in his cage by her feet.

"What is it?" she asked the fox.

"I caught this one sneaking around beyond the wil-
low trees," the fox replied. "He was looking for a way in."

Two dryads marched into the grove and threw the
stranger to his knees before the throne.

The stranger looked up and saw Gerardo. It had
been less than a year, but Gerardo looked like he'd
aged a decade since the stranger last saw him. His long,
raven-feather hair was now streaked with silver.

"Hello," Gerardo said from inside the cage. "What're you doing here?"

"I came to save you," the stranger told him.

The madman considered the situation.

"That'll be a neat trick," he said. "I can't wait to see it."

Sometimes you just need a little lighthearted faith.

THE CHASE

At her court in the fey realm, Brigidde the Bright One sat on her throne and contemplated her prisoner.

The stranger's hands were bound, and he was forced to kneel before the queen.

Gerardo looked on with concern from his cage.

"I believe we shall have some entertainment!" Brigidde now called. She clapped her hands. "Come Niall! Come Kilian! Come Eamon!"

The red fox sat up at her feet. Meanwhile, a white-bellied stoat scampered closer from the edge of the grove and a peregrine falcon swooped from the trees to land on the back of her throne.

The queen clapped again and suddenly, crouched in Gerardo's place, was a small, white rabbit.

"You know the rules, Gerardo darling," Brigidde said. "If you survive the hour, you will be returned to your human shape. Good luck."

She kicked open the cage.

Gerardo sprang forth and bolted from the grove.

With a flutter of wings and a rush of grass, the three hunters gave chase.

"Watch carefully," Brigidde told the stranger. "You're next."

⇒⇒⇒⇒ ⇐⇐⇐⇐

Watch and learn from the trials of those around you.

THE SCHOLAR AND THE SPELLSLINGER

The first time the spellslinger mage came to Adain's office, she didn't know what to expect.

She had read his books and his papers. She knew beyond a doubt that he had been through the void to other worlds. She suspected that he had been there, on her homeworld, when the Empress was killed.

She thought he might be a warrior.

But though the man she met had a grim scar down one side of his face, his bearing was not that of a soldier.

Adain looked up from his papers as the spellslinger mage stood in the doorway.

He examined her and said, "You look like someone I know. A dangerous stranger."

"You look like someone with a secret," she said. "I wonder whether you'll tell it to me. How did you survive the whirlpool gate?"

Adain hesitated. Once, back when he lived in Ghenkis, he might have claimed credit for the feat. Or insisted he had some special knowledge. That was how it was, between the backstabbing academics of the Old College where he had been trained.

Instead, though, he shrugged. "You haven't met my friends," he said. "They're the only reason I survived."

The spellslinger raised one eyebrow. Her eyes were bright as copper pennies. "If they're so special, why did your friends need you along?"

Adain shrugged again. But this time he gave a little grin.

"They might be able to survive. But I'm the only one with the skill to tell the tale."

The spellslinger mage sat down across the desk. "Alright then," she said. "Tell it to me."

So Adain told her the story, and told it well.

Afterwards, she decided not to kill him.

Be honest about your weaknesses. Be confident in your strengths.

THE WORN CLOAK

Brigidde, queen among the fairies, clapped her hands and cheered gleefully when the white rabbit darted across her grove and back into its cage.

The red fox was just behind, panting and drooling.

But the cage snapped shut in his face.

"Ah ah!" Brigidde scolded. "The hour is up. Your prey has escaped you."

She clapped again and, in the cage, the white rabbit changed back into Gerardo.

"But there's always next time..." the queen said. And she turned to the stranger.

The dryads had taken the stranger's old sword when they captured him. All they left him were his scuffed boots and threadbare cloak.

He stood before the queen, defenseless.

"Ready to run?" she asked, grinning her bright, fey grin.

The stranger stared back, watching her with his copper penny eyes.

Brigidde clapped her hands.

A sudden hush fell throughout the grove.

There was a white rabbit seated on the throne.

The stranger tugged at the frayed hem of his cloak.

"This was woven by my people's finest spellweavers," he explained to Gerardo, bending down to unfasten the cage. "From fibers of the trees in the Field of Souls. Designed to protect the wearer and ward off evil magic."

Gerardo looked stunned. "Did you know that would happen?" he mumbled, crawling out of the cage and stretching his limbs.

"I hoped it might," the stranger said. "Now, how about we get you home?"

Believe in what you've been given.

THE WELCOME HOME

G erardo and the stranger hobbled from the hills and down the dusty road into Josek.

The town was bigger than either of them remembered. Since they closed the whirlpool gate under the mountains, settlers had been flooding in.

When the mayor heard that they had returned, she sent deputies to escort them to her rooms at the new hotel. She looked different, handsomely dressed in a tasseled buckskin jacket and knee-high riding boots.

"It's good to see you," she said. "I'm glad you're safe." She grasped the stranger's hand warmly, and pulled Gerardo into a hug.

Gerardo stiffened, then relaxed. For the last year, he had been trapped in the land of the fey — the plaything of a powerful fairy queen. It was good to be home, and among comrades again.

The mayor stepped back. Her stormy blue eyes met the stranger's copper ones. "One of your people is here," she said. "A spellslinger mage. She's been awaiting your return."

He nodded. "It was inevitable, I suppose. All of my kindred felt the moment we killed the Empress. They will want answers."

"Whatever they want," the mayor said, and now she smiled, "it can wait until after you've both bathed." She gestured to the door of the washroom. "Welcome home."

"Home..." the stranger mused as he washed the dust and sweat from his body. He hadn't had one of those in a long time.

❧❧❧ ❦❦❦

Home means peace and stability. But don't expect your home to remain unchanged. There will always be something new waiting for us when we return.

THE SACRIFICE

When the stranger and the spellslinger mage met in Josek, it was not for the first time.

They came to earth five thousand years ago with their kindred, sailing together on ships between the stars, and their arrival laid low the civilizations of men. In the wake of their devastation, they parted ways, promising to wander the ruins until they had righted the wrongs they brought upon this place.

The two met again in the office of Adain, the scarred scholar, who had followed the stranger through the whirlpool gate to right those wrongs.

The spellslinger mage was angry.

"You brought strangers to the Field of Souls," she accused him. "Our most sacred place. And they burned it to the ground. I felt the tremors when they killed the Empress. They left our world in ruins."

"You didn't see it," the stranger protested. He approached her.

Her hand twitched toward her wand, slung in a holster at her waist.

"Look," he told her. "See what I saw."

The stranger gripped her forearm and Adain saw tendrils like tiny roots erupt from his hands. They burrowed into her bare skin and the spellslinger's eyes rolled up in her head. Her body shuddered as dozens of memories passed through her mind.

"The Empress was not who she had been," the stranger murmured hoarsely. "The Praeds had already corrupted her, turned her into a warped shadow of her former self. She was not our mother any longer."

He released the mage and stepped back, lowering his eyes to the floor. "We could not save her."

The spellslinger struggled for breath. A tear rolled down her face as she collected herself.

"But you closed the whirlpool gate," she admitted. "The Praeds are trapped beyond, on a world that cannot sustain them forever. The plague that tore our people apart will die with them. And there will be no more demons here."

The stranger nodded.

The mage sank down in a chair by the hearth. "It still hurts," she said.

They sat together, and only the crackling fire made a sound.

Accept the sacrifice you've made to get here. Honor it. It was necessary.

THE TOAST

Inez the fireman arrived at the town of Josek in the borderlands carrying twigs, seeds and clippings of a sacred tree from the northernmost mountains.

In Josek, she found the scarred scholar, Adain.

"I was told to bring these to you," she said. "And I do it to honor a great debt. I would not have escaped those mountains if it wasn't for your friend, Dolf."

Adain coughed and dabbed at his eyes. "Tell me the tale," he said after a moment of quiet.

When she was done, Inez lit the fire with a wave of her hand while Adain went over to the cabinet. He took down an old bottle.

"We don't drink to forget," he said, pouring two glasses and raising one of them, "but to do honor. A toast: to friends, comrades and grumpy old firemen named Dolf."

"To comrades," Inez said. She cracked a smile. "And to Dolf."

They both drank.

Honor each other, even in memory, because the seeds we plant are not ours but came to us through great sacrifice.

THE NEW GROWTH

Of course, Adain told the stranger as soon as Inez the fireman had left his office.

"She came with a message from Dolf," Adain said. "And these."

The stranger examined the seeds and twigs. His copper eyes widened. "These are from the Empress, the mother tree of my homeworld. How did she acquire them?"

"Inez says they found a sapling far to the north, in the mountains of the Aghoori Hordes. The tree seemed to be fueling the enemy's sorcerers, so they burned it to cinders, but not before Dolf took clippings. We've long suspected the Hordes are consorting with demons from your home world. I imagine that some Aghoori, many generations ago, must have journeyed through the whirlpool gate to your home and retrieved a sample."

The stranger clutched the seeds in his hand. "I had thought the Empress was dead, and the future of my race along with it. But now..." His eyes gleamed. "All life on my world sprang from the mother tree. She grows slowly, but if she lives long enough... There is yet hope for my people."

They planted the seeds on a hill in the wilderness beyond Josek. Gerardo chose the spot. The mayor of Josek declared the place a land trust for miles in every direction. Adain built himself a cabin in the woods, to watch over the project. His students grew used to visiting him there for their lessons.

The stranger and the spellslinger mage took turns standing guard over the single green sprout that pierced the soil. By night, they sang old songs in their haunting, alien language, and offered sacred prayers.

Slowly, the tree grew.

Where there is growth, there is hope.

THE HIDDEN TREASURE

One night, the spellslinger mage came upon a man in the darkness of the garden. He had a spade in his hands, and was digging desperately at the roots of the sacred tree.

The man spun around in the dark and dove for his crossbow.

But her wand twitched from its holster. A bolt of light cut him down like a marionette.

The mayor of Josek would not prosecute.

"It's trespassing," she said. "And intent to commit robbery."

The people of Josek were outraged.

"The mage is a stranger here," they protested. "Not even one of us. And we've all heard the rumors. Their secret garden is full of gold and jewels, plundered from the graves of our ancestors in the mountains. That's why no one is allowed to visit."

In vain, the mayor tried to quell the crowds.

They gathered torches and weapons. They went out into the woods, hunting, hungry for justice.

Adain, the scarred scholar who lived in the hills near the garden, saw them from a long way off.

"Too many to fight," he told the mage. "If they have their way, they'll burn this whole place to the ground."

When the mob arrived, Adain allowed them to search the walled garden. But the mage was gone. So was Adain's cart. So was the tree.

The people searched the forest, but they were nowhere to be found.

⇶ ⇇

You do not have to fight. Force cannot conquer ignorance.

THE PAST

"Does it ever seem like a dream?" asked Adain.

The woman gave him a long, slow look. Her dark skin was unlined, but her long hair was streaked with silver. She was no longer the mayor of Josek. Some people, the ones who had known her a long time, still thought of her as the sheriff.

Adain did, anyway.

Her stormy blue gaze lingered on his face, where the long scar cut across one eye. It was nearly fifty years since they had passed through the whirlpool gate with the stranger, and Adain had earned that scar. "It wasn't a dream," she said at last.

"I just wonder..." Adain trailed off. "Do you think he's still out there? After all this time?"

The sheriff gave the scholar another look. She knew he was talking about the stranger. "He's out there," she said. "He's a tough one to kill. And long as we remember him, he can't die."

﹥﹥﹥ ﹤﹤﹤

The connections we make are not bounded by space and time. They last as long as we nurture them.

THE OFFERING

The stranger came for Gerardo one night, just after sunset.

"Follow me," he said, and Gerardo followed his friend into the night.

They took a shortcut through the realm of the fey, where none dared to hinder them. They emerged on a windswept plateau far to the west.

The spellslinger mage stood nearby. She nodded to Gerardo, but he didn't reply. The madman was captivated by the third shadow that loomed in the moonlight.

The tree was still young, but she was beautiful. She rose forty feet into the sky, sprouting lithe branches covered scantly by modest leaves. On one of the lowest branches, a plump fruit hung temptingly.

"This is the first fruit of the mother tree," said the stranger. "Our legends say that the first fruit grants wisdom and immortality to those who taste it."

He plucked the fruit, holding it reverently. Then, he turned to Gerardo. He held out his hands.

"You were my first friend," the stranger said. "And I know no one more pure in spirit."

Gerardo accepted the offering. He hesitated only a moment. "Are the legends true?" he asked.

The stranger and the spellslinger shared a look.

"I don't know about any wisdom," the stranger said. "But we're still here."

Gerardo laughed. Then he sank his teeth into the fruit, and sweet juice ran down his chin.

Life offers incredible gifts to those who prove worthy of them.

THE FRIEND

From the southern desert, a stranger arrived in Josek. He wore old boots and a tattered cloak that billowed in the dusty wind. And he carried a sword at his hip, a worn sword that had never been hung over the mantlepiece.

Only his eyes were new. Like bright copper pennies, or the sun shining suddenly on your face.

He came to Josek again, twice more, to be with Adain and the sheriff when they passed through the veil.

Only on these occasions, he did not come as a stranger. He came as their friend.

They knew him, and felt glad he was there.

⟫⟫⟫ ⟪⟪⟪

Friendship changes everything. Friendship is the seed of love.

ABOUT THE AUTHOR

Jack Dolinar is a writer who believes that the positive ripples we create have an impact far larger than we can comprehend. He is passionate about bringing action-able wisdom into everyday life, for himself and those around him.

ARCHIVES is his second work of wisdom literature.

You can find his other writing at jackdolinar.com.